SUNDAY MORNING AT THE CENTRE OF THE WORLD

Louis de Bernières is the author of *Red Dog* (2001), and four other novels: *The War of Don Emmanuel's Nether Parts* (Commonwealth Writers Prize, Best First Book Eurasia Region, 1991), *Señor Vivo and the Coca Lord* (Commonwealth Writers Prize, Best Book Eurasia Region, 1992), *The Troublesome Offspring of Cardinal Guzman*, and *Captain Corelli's Mandolin* (Commonwealth Writers Prize, Best Book, 1995).

ALSO BY LOUIS DE BERNIERES

The War of Don Emmanuel's Nether Parts

Señor Vivo and the Coca Lord

The Troublesome Offspring of Cardinal Guzman

Captain Corelli's Mandolin

Red Dog

The War of Don Emmanuel's Nether Parts:

'A very good book indeed, the sharpest and funniest I have read in quite some time'
Financial Times

'A fat, juicy tropical fruit of a narrative . . . There is astonishing landscape. There are numerous good jokes. And, indispensably in such a novel, there is magic'
Independent on Sunday

'A wonderful mixture of the mythical and poetic, of the cruel and clinical aspects of life . . . I have seldom read a finer first novel. It is one to savour and revisit'
Scotland on Sunday

'A tour de force' *Time Out*

Señor Vivo and the Coca Lord:

'Virbrant, lucid, charged with wild jokes and harrowing scenes smelted with torture . . . A book which shudders with memorability . . . Satirical and splendid'
Scotland on Sunday

'Sharp, funny, engaging and British . . . de Bernières is doing for Colombia's drug culture what Tom Sharpe did for apartheid. His approach is flippant, but the purpose behind it is deadly serious'
Financial Times

The Troublesome Offspring of Cardinal Guzman:

'A novel of prodigious imagination'
Scotland on Sunday

'A carnival of pain and pleasure, violence, tenderness, high jinks of every sexual sort, quaint customs and quainter jokes'
Financial Times

'An extraordinary feat of imagination . . . A sensuous, often farcical and ultimately optimistic argument for spiritual sanity'
Time Out

Louis de Bernières

SUNDAY MORNING AT THE CENTRE OF THE WORLD

A PLAY FOR VOICES

First broadcast on BBC radio 1998
Performed at the Dylan Thomas Centre,
Swansea, in 1999 and 2000

VINTAGE

Published by Vintage 2001

4 6 8 10 9 7 5

A Vintage Original

Vintage
Random House, 20 Vauxhall Bridge Road,
London SW1V 2SA

Random House Australia (Pty) Limited
20 Alfred Street, Milsons Point, Sydney,
New South Wales 2061, Australia

Random House New Zealand Limited
18 Poland Road, Glenfield,
Auckland 10, New Zealand

Random House (Pty) Limited
Endulini, 5A Jubilee Road, Parktown 2193, South Africa

The Random House Group Limited Reg. No. 954009
www.randomhouse.co.uk

A CIP catalogue record for this book
is available from the British Library

ISBN 0 09 942844 X

Set in 11½/14 Sabon by SX Composing DTP, Rayleigh, Essex
Printed and bound in Great Britain by Cox & Wyman Ltd, Reading, Berkshire

FOREWORD

This work ostensibly began life as a radio play, commissioned in 1998 by Kate McAll for Radio 4, but in fact its genesis goes back a considerable way. In the first place, I had decided to leave Earlsfield, a part of South West London where I had lived for about ten years. I had been living above a small shop on Garratt Lane that had been by turns an outlet for oversized naughty clothes for transvestites, a West Indian hairdressers, and a junk shop.

I had first moved to Earlsfield in order to be within walking distance of a teaching job that I promptly lost, yet I stayed there for a decade despite my yearning to get back to the countryside whence I came. During that time I had my longest relationship, adopted a cat (despite having been initially appalled at the thought of such awesome responsibility), and gradually transformed myself from a very depressed and impoverished supply teacher with no future, into a reasonably successful writer with four novels under his belt and an enviably idle lifestyle.

I also got to know my neighbours very well, a process simplified by previous experience working as a car mechanic in a very dodgy garage in Stoke Newington, and by my years working in London schools. My voice quite unconsciously lost the 'posh' accent it had grown up with, and recently I was surprised to see the *Irish Times* describe me as a cockney, just when I had reconciled myself to being incurably middle-class, and some fifteen years after I had given up my regret for not being the working-class hero whose affectation was *de rigueur* to the dismal youth of the 1970s.

I have, therefore, no pretensions to any 'street-cred' whatsoever, and moreover I don't think that anyone who has lived with working-class people would really be tempted to romanticise them for very long; they are as humorous, bigoted, churlish or kind as any other sort of person. I wrote this because I had grown very fond of my neighbours, wanting both to remember them, and to celebrate my life alongside them. Many of them had been in my side-street since before the war, and now all but one of those old people has died of smoking-related diseases. My most heart-rending memory is of receiving a desperate phone call from an old lady who was unable to lift her emphysemic husband from the lavatory. He had been a huge foundry worker from Ulster, of the 'bitter proddy' variety, but by then he looked like a victim of Belsen. He had sticking plasters over the places where his bones were coming through his skin, and I could lift him with one arm. I am thankful that I got to know him and the others whilst there was still time, and I am glad that some of their voices are refracted through these pages. There is in fact almost nothing fictional in the anecdotes and stories told here, and all the voices have their real counterparts.

People have often remarked that I am one of those writers who always sets their work abroad. In reality I have set quite a number of stories in England, but they have never been published in a collection. However, there is a sense in which *Sunday Morning at the Centre of the World* is set as much abroad as any of my novels. A middle-class boy from rural Surrey is as much a foreigner in Earlsfield as the person who arrives from Ireland, unless he is the kind who has bought his first house, stays only a couple of years, never meets his neighbours, and then buys a bigger house nearer to somewhere 'nice'. There were always lots of these, and I never got to know any of them. They are a kind of ghost that flits through the lives of those who sit on the wall and chat. If, however, you are the kind of person who has a popular cat and works out in the street on his own car, you will inevitably be drawn into the ambit of local joke and gossip, and you will rapidly become a neighbour in the proper sense of the word.

To go back further, however, it will be clear to anyone that I have taken my inspiration from *Under Milk Wood*. I was lucky as a boy in having a succession of inspirational English teachers, and one day one of them pushed open the door of the classroom with his foot, and came in carrying a mono record player with a record on top. He had the infectious air of one who has made a wonderful discovery that he wishes to share, and we spent a double lesson entranced by the voices of Richard Burton and the rest of the cast. Dylan Thomas had the ability to make the English language sound completely new, a side-effect of his sense of humour and his very idiosyncratic literary style, and this one schoolroom experience was to have a profound effect upon me; it was a further step into the love-affair with the English language that I have been conducting all my life. At about the same time my younger sister suddenly became a Dylan Thomas fan, and took to reciting 'Fern Hill' at the slightest provocation. I bought her the complete poems as a present, but, of course, first read through the book myself.

I am not a poet, although I often wish that I were, and so I have not attempted any special effects to equal those of Dylan Thomas. The most obvious similarity between *Sunday Morning* and *Under Milk Wood* is in the use of the voices of the dead. I am a great wanderer around cemeteries, I frequently feel tearful upon reading the more poignant epitaphs, and from time to time I like to confront my mortality in a suitably romantic and morbid fashion.

One can discern the history of a community by following the succession of names on the stones; in Earlsfield cemetery there are the great tombs of Victorian bourgeois, and war graves of Australians who died of wounds upon returning from Gallipoli. One can place the arrival of Poles and West Indians. One can tell when young women stopped dying in childbed, one can tell when it was that young men started to die in motorcycle crashes, and again when it was that they started to die of drugs. There was another graveyard nearby containing the bones of Huguenots, the people from whom I am descended. I am wedded to the idea that the dead are as much a part of a community as the living, something that perhaps Dylan Thomas also felt. If I were dead, but still aware, I would be frustrated at not being able to address the living, and so I let the dead of Earlsfield speak.

This piece is my farewell embrace to the polymorphous people of Earlsfield, with whom I lived for ten years before finally making the leap of faith that took me back out into the countryside. Certainly I do not miss the noise and stink of Garratt Lane, nor the sheer torment of having to use public transport in an overcrowded city. Out in the country I am less easy to get at, and so I have more peace and quiet. I can work underneath my car without lying in dogshit or having to put my tools away every time I go indoors. It is fortunate, however, that nowadays even little country towns have tandooris, Chinese takeaways, and 'Paki' shops that are open till midnight. Urban blacks are beginning to filter outwards too, and so the London refugee such as myself does not necessarily feel any strong sense of loss or exile. Even so, ten years is a large slice of life, and I am happy that it is easy to go back whenever I wish.

Sunday Morning at the Centre of the World was broadcast twice by the BBC, as was customary, and then there was a period in which I feared that it would sink without trace. It was, however, picked up by the poet, Dave Woolley of the Dylan Thomas Centre in Swansea, who had it enacted there in 1999, and again in 2000. On the second occasion I was the narrator, and I was pleasantly surprised at how well it worked when performed live. It is thanks to the extra lease of life that Dave Woolley has given it that I have been encouraged to weave in much material that occurred to me in the months following its original broadcast, and which I wrote down originally in a kind of pseudo-verse.

Obviously this work is dedicated to the living and dead of Earlsfield, which was definitely the centre of the world when I was living in it. It must also be dedicated to the shade of Dylan Thomas and to Kate McAll who commissioned the play in the first place.

SUNDAY MORNING AT THE CENTRE OF THE WORLD

NARRATOR

It is early in the morning, Sunday, and Posh
Katy sings in the bath. Her cool contralto
negotiates the louvres, is filtered by the leaves
of hornbeam, and glides above the broken
tiles and peeling sills of almost-sunny, always-
grubby, never-uppity Earlsfield at the centre of
the world.

POSH KATY
(*singing*)

Everybody got that fever
That is something you all know
Fever isn't such a nuisance
Fever started long ago
You give me fever
When you kiss me
Fever when you hold me tight
Fever!
In the morning
Fever all through the night . . . .

Posh Katy splashes and sings, and up in the bedroom the no-good boyfriend snores away the seconds. He will wake up when his tea is exactly the right temperature, but now he dreams of going to a shop and not remembering what it was he came to buy.

Posh Katy sings 'Never knew how much I love you . . .' and above the rooftops her voice mingles with that of Mr Wong, inveterate gambler, Chinese fish-and-chippie, fan of Pavarotti. Mr Wong sings along with Luciano.

MR WONG
(*singing*)

Che berra cosa
'na iurnata'e soray
n'alia selena
doppo 'na tempesta . . .

NARRATOR

Mrs Wong rolls out of bed, hears her husband warbling as he shaves, feels suddenly tired, and rolls back under the sheet. She sleeps again, in a reverie of palm-oil, steak and kidney pie, codfish and rock, ketchup and salt, Jamaica pattie and plaice. Mrs Wong serves her chips in her sleep and asks as normal

MRS WONG

Open or lapped?

NARRATOR

Mrs Wong, twenty years a chippie, knows that Brits are vile. They are drunk and sneering when the dark pubs close, and pour artificial vinegar on their chips. In her sleep she cries

MRS WONG

Hollible! Hollible!

NARRATOR

Who but barbarians would put vinegar on chips? Again she cries

MRS WONG

Hollible! Hollible!

NARRATOR

The voices of Mr Wong and Katy mingle in song above the gutters and the dirty roofs.

MR WONG AND POSH KATY
(*singing*)

Never knew how much I love you . . . O soray mio, sta 'nfronte a te . . . Never know how much I care . . . O soray, o soray mio . . . When you put your arms around me . . . sta 'nfronte a te . . . I get a fever that's a-hard to bear.

NARRATOR

Potty Ingrid throws open the sash and slings out bread that falls like rubber snow amid the dustbins and the ragged robin that grows in cracks, and the hawkweed and convolvulus and the chip-wrappers and the drying evidence of the last night's drunks.

POTTY INGRID

Come on my darlings! My pretty ones! My sweets! My bright-eyed babies!

NARRATOR

And down fly the feral doves, unbowed but battered and tattered, martyrs to mites, their guts in permanent flux from their orgies of chips and bread and burger buns, their birdseed and roadgrit and water floating with oil.

POTTY INGRID

Come on, my darlings!

NARRATOR

Potty Ingrid, her hair in knots, slams down the

sash, and the three black cats of Ramillies Road spring out from behind the wall, the hedge, the bin. There used to be fifty-one pigeons, but now there's only ten.

POTTY INGRID

I wonder where all my darlings are.

NARRATOR

This is the praise and thanks of the three black cats of Ramillies Road.

THE THREE BLACK CATS

Thanks be to Potty Ingrid, our gracious lady,
Who gives us our daily birds,
With crunchy bones and sweet warm blood,
And feathers that stick in our teeth.
Forgive us our yowlings
And save us from fleabites and dogs.

NARRATOR

Potty Ingrid strokes her terrier, legs like toothpicks, coat like a janitor's mop, and asks it a serious question:

POTTY INGRID

Darling, do you think I'm eccentric?

NARRATOR

The dog affirms with a wag of the stump, and the London sparrows bounce on the sills and sing:

THE LONDON SPARROWS

Tweet bloody tweet!

NARRATOR

The urban foxes, smart and respectable, stir in their sleep in their burrows by graves, and the clay of the dead melds with the roots of grass and trees, and their voices are stirring the stones.

THE VOICES OF THE DEAD

First Voice: I remember.
Second Voice: It wasn't like this before.
Third Voice: Never had to lock.
First Voice: A green field and a wood.
Second Voice: No bloody foreigners.
Third Voice: Everyone in and out, just like that.
First Voice: At the end of the street.
Second Voice: Suet pudding.
Third Voice: Borrowing sugar.
First Voice: Promise I'll bring it back.
Second Voice: When the cows come home.
Third Voice: Songs in the pub.
First Voice: The old Joanna.

Second Voice: Foam in the river, up to the
bridge, all crested in brown. It was pretty, that
was.
Third Voice: River's all clean.
First Voice: Disgraceful, I call it.
All the Voices: It wasn't like this before.
First Voice: What did you die of then?
Second Voice: Nothing much. Just death really.
Third Voice: Well, there's worse things to die of
than that.

NARRATOR

And here comes Ethel, prime surveyor of news
and views, with her lavender rinse, her pink-
rimmed specs, her Mills and Boon, her one
snout daily, gingham bag and practical shoes.

ETHEL

'Ello, darlin', how are you?
Bin ages, innit?
Bin hidin' somewhere, 'ave you?
'Ere, I saw your Toby
Sittin' on next door's wall;
He's a great one, that one is.
Did yer hear what happened to Suzie?
Only died last week,
It was heartbreaking,
God it was,
And I ain't recovered,
Don't ever reckon I would.

Nah,
She wa'n't bowled down by a car,
It was somefink went wrong in her brain,
And she upped and died like that,
All in a terrible fit, and
She was lovely that one was, but
That's the trouble with cats;
Always breaking your heart.

NARRATOR

Parachute Sam, elite but unemployed, with his
brains at all degrees and his fusewire hair, with
his red beret and his khaki fatigues, his durable
moulded soles all bulled-up and buffed,
swaggers and struts the Foreign Legion march
up Ramillies Road and Fantasy Lane. Before
breakfast he has pulled off lightning raids; freed
hostages, and foiled the foreign powers.
Parachute Sam reads magazines, knows the
secrets of martial art, is expert with every
weapon, survives at the poles and at the centre
of the sun, makes porridge with grass and
burgers with worms, does unarmed combat in
mirrors and shopfront glass. Today he has
bushed his moustached, has suppressed a rising
of Arabs in the desert of Fantasy Lane, and
proceeds up Ramillies Road to the Foreign
Legion march.

Gauche droite, gauche droite, gauche droite . . .

NARRATOR

And the London Sparrows go 'Tweet effin'
tweet', and Posh Katy sings 'Fever', and Mrs
Wong goes 'Hollible, hollible' and the voices of
the dead say 'Thank God I didn't live to see it
as it is today'.

Athwart the low wall are Thrombotic Bert and
Emphysemic Eric, watching the line of cars that
queue for the boot in the school. Thrombotic
Bert observes

THROMBOTIC BERT

There goes Parachute Sam.

EMPHYSEMIC ERIC

Silly sod.

THROMBOTIC BERT

I heard you got emphasyemicwotsit. Smokin'
that did it, was it?

EMPHYSEMIC ERIC

Can't be; I stopped two weeks ago.

THROMBOTIC BERT

That's bad luck then. Gotta 'ave an operation?

EMPHYSEMIC ERIC

Nah, I just got a bloody great tank of oxygen.

THROMBOTIC BERT

You're alright for weldin' then. Did I tell you what happened this morning? Right? I was lookin' out my window, right? The one over Garratt Lane, and I sees all these slappers lined up against the wall, like. Rough or what? Bloody 'ell. They were rough. A right bunch of dogs. Roughest birds I seen since I don't know when. Miniskirts and big white thighs, like that, boatraces all covered with zits and hair with the roots showin', all bleached with Domestos, and lips red like a sodding vampire. Blimey. So I calls my wife and I says ''Ere, take a look at this' and she comes to the window and I says 'Look at all them effin' prozzies. Where'd they come from all of sudden? We ain't never 'ad tarts like that 'til now.' And she looks at me and she shakes 'er 'ead, and she says, 'Those ain't no prozzies. Those is our neighbours, and that's a temporary bus stop.' 'Bloody 'ell,' I says, 'reckon I need a new pair of specs.'

My old lady was waiting for the 77. She says you was gawping from the window. Give us a fag. I'll give up again later. Don't tell the wife, like.

THROMBOTIC BERT

Don't do you any harm anyway, I don't think. I had an uncle right? And he smoked ninety a day, right? And he got to ninety-nine years old, and never a day's illness. And if it's so bad, why do all them nurses smoke so much, that's what I want to know. Doctor reckons it was fags and fry-ups wot did my legs in, but I reckon 'e was talkin' through his you-know-wotsit. They don't know nothing, they just think they do.

EMPHYSEMIC ERIC

Why didn't he get to a hundred, then, this uncle?

THROMBOTIC BERT

He died, didn't he? That's why.

EMPHYSEMIC ERIC

Just wondered, that's all.

THROMBOTIC BERT

Here, if you got one moth ball in this hand, and one moth ball in that hand, what've you got?

EMPHYSEMIC ERIC

I dunno. What? Two mothballs?

THROMBOTIC BERT

No. A bloody great moth.

EMPHYSEMIC ERIC

Silly sod.

NARRATOR

Two blue plastic carrier bags waltz together on the wind above the shops, twirling and dipping, soaring and lifting, courtly-dancing on the breeze of Garratt Lane. Thrombotic Bert and Emphysemic Eric are sitting on the low wall, dragging their fags, regarding.

THROMBOTIC BERT

It's those two bleeding bags again.

EMPHYSEMIC ERIC

Every day, always the same, the same blue bags, wafting away to Tooting Bec.

12

THROMBOTIC BERT

How do they get back? That's what I want to
know.

EMPHYSEMIC ERIC

What do they do in Tooting Bec?

THROMBOTIC BERT

Waft about, mate, waft ableedingbout.

NARRATOR

Deathwish Debbie, tall and slim, her hair in
tufts and tiny plaits, in everyday disguise
(combat boots and khaki, navel-nose-and-
ear-and-lip-pierced, lovely as a new rose, if
only) spots Kevin the Dealer and her feet fly
to meet him. Round his neck her arms are
flung, and their lips lock in the holy image of
a filmstar kiss. Antique Annie, hobbling past,
remembers him she loved before the war,
saying goodbye, kissing farewell forever for
too-short-a-time by the train at Waterloo,
swathed in fear, desire, and a fog of steam, in
a world that reeked of coal and sodden
dented hopes.

I've had my chance, I was young like them, no grounds to grumble. But it's sad even though I feel glad, to see the young, the young in love. If only I was young.

NARRATOR

But Deathwish Debbie is out of the reach of love. In Kevin the Dealer's pockets are Debbie's banknotes, and in her mouth is the crack their kiss exchanged. Deathwish Debbie will be happy, will be God, down the alley, behind the bins, with her friends, but not for long, drowning in bliss, smoke wreathing from cans, blazing like stars, dancing the Graveyard Fling.

DEATHWISH DEBBIE

I'll have to go on the game. How else can I pay? It's the only way. O Christ, I'll have to go on the game. Save me. Don't save me. I've got to have some. I've got to stop. It's the last time, but just once more, O Christ, I'll have to go on the game.

NARRATOR

In the impotence of death, the bones cry out from beneath the turf, the drunken stones, the broken stones, and the soil that's salt with years.

First Voice: Don't do it, Debs. Please love, don't.

Second Voice: It ain't worf it.

Third Voice: You're young and pretty.

First Voice: Life before you.

Second Voice: Not like us.

Third Voice: Muscles and blood. You don't know how lucky you are.

First Voice: Nothing to do down here.

Second Voice: It was gin killed me.

Third Voice: And now you ain't got lips.

First Voice: This Irish skeleton, he goes into a pub, right? And he goes up to the bar, and he says to the barman, 'I'll 'ave a pint of Guinness and a mop.'

ALL THREE VOICES
(*singing*)

I ain't got no body . . .

NARRATOR

Thrombotic Bert and Emphysemic Eric slouch on the wall, and the fagends fall at their feet and expire. Antique Annie, legs a-tired and feet too hot, plumps herself down and sighs.

ANTIQUE ANNIE

'Ere, did you 'ear what 'appened to 'Arry?

THROMBOTIC BERT AND EMPHYSEMIC ERIC

Nah. What did?

ANTIQUE ANNIE

Got mugged, didn't he? He's black and blue all over.

THROMBOTIC BERT

Bloody 'ell, that's terrible.

EMPHYSEMIC ERIC

Terrible.

ANTIQUE ANNIE

Terrible, innit? It's a right disgrace. And you know what? 'E only 'ad 50p. They only went and mugged 'im for 50 bleedin' p.

NARRATOR

The three fall quiet and gaze at the ground, their sighs of loss like falling leaves, and Annie speaks for them all:

16

There wasn't any violence during the war.

NARRATOR

And the vehicles of Garratt Lane raise the fine dark dust that comes in through window frames, curls through keyholes, rises through boards, settles on tables and trinkets, seasons the food, dries out the eyes, lines the lungs, gets in the works, clogs the disc-drive, bedevils the duster, and mats the hair of the head. Earlsfield dreams in the cardust as the Catholics drift from St Gregory's into God's congregation for the Wandle River boot.

Here be pitted chisels,

ALL CAST MEMBERS,
A LINE AT A TIME EACH

LPs of Los Trio Paraguayos with a scratch on both sides,
Silverplated forks and spoons with the plate worn off,
Dinted lamps,
Chess sets with the white knight gone,
Brushes set sempiternal in cloggedy off-white paint,
Manuals for cars Great Uncle drove,
Clothes of man-made cloth in heaps of multi-hue,

17

Unhappy house-plants,
Anachronistic maps,
Novels with decent chaps and spunky slim-
hipped girls,
Toys without batteries,
Blowlamps without washers,
Sets of plugless Lo-Fi,
Dead men's shoes,
One-handed breast pumps,
Bricabracbroken,
Porcelain gewgaws and brass buggeralls,
Wooden nothings and Bakelite blimeywhat's-
thats,
And assorted I-don't-know-mate-you-tell-mes.

And here be Poles who mend your watch.
Here be Muslim girls with pretty red shoes,
veiled to the nines in black.
Here be Osties, purveyors of communist tat,
Here be Turks, taking time off from the caff.
Here be Greeks, far-wandering,
Here be blacks panafrican, and
Here be blacks West Indian, and
Here be fat slags with blue tattoos and foul
mouths, and
Here be pretty blondes who lean on cars,
and
Here be white girls with café crème kids, and
Here be hot dogs, and
Here be Spaniards with London mouths, and
Here be French who came by mistake, and
Here be children grasping at toys, and

Here be a man with a big beard and a tweed
hat, and
Here be the Paddy with a kind word, and
Here be the Taffy with a red face, and
Here be Rastas pickled in smoke, and
Here be the Scot with common sense, and
Here be the Paki who's a witness for Jehovah,
and
Here be Mohammeds and Singhs and things,
and
Here be pigeons, and
Here be Persians, sad for home, and
Here be Iraquis, sad for home, and
Here be Somalis, sad for home, and
Here be Bosnians, sad for home, and
Here be Thais and pretty Filipinas, and
Here be Mrs Patel, the Earlsfield belle,
With her work-roughed hands, and
Her angel's smile and her delicate bones, and
Her mischievous eyes, and
Here be the Earlsfield intelligentsia, and
Here be couples in love and
Here be pushchairs that block the aisles, and

ALL THE CAST TOGETHER

Here be the Babel that made the city new.

POTTY INGRID

I got it for a quid. You can have it for 75p. I
only used it once.

19

ANTIQUE ANNIE

Nice, isn't it? Gawd knows what it's for.

THROMBOTIC BERT

Put it down, Missus, you can't afford it.

ANTIQUE ANNIE AND INGRID
(*together*)

Cheeky sod.

ANTIQUE ANNIE

I'll give you 50p.

POTTY INGRID

Oh alright, go on then. It's got some knobs missing.

NARRATOR

Here also be unsuccessful deals.

FIRST ANONYMOUS VOICE

I'll give yer three pound fifty.

SECOND ANONYMOUS VOICE

I said five pounds.

FIRST ANONYMOUS VOICE

Four pounds.

SECOND ANONYMOUS VOICE

I said five pounds.

FIRST ANONYMOUS VOICE

Four pounds fifty.

SECOND ANONYMOUS VOICE

Look, ain't that worth five pounds? It's five pounds, alright? I got rent to pay.

FIRST ANONYMOUS VOICE

Listen mate, I like haggling, but not when the other bloke won't budge his price.

SECOND ANONYMOUS VOICE

Well, it ain't haggling then, is it?

NARRATOR

Here also be excellent advice.

THIRD ANONYMOUS VOICE

I tripped over, I did, and that was me, flat on me face, and I said to Dave, I did, I said, why d'yer have to leave your stuff all over the bleedin' floor? And I tell yer what, I ain't been the same since, and me wrist still hurts, and yer know what? I went to the Brocklebank Health Centre, Brocklewank more like, and I waited two soddin' hours 'til I got fed up, and I came home cause it was tea, and now it don't arf bleedin' throb.

FOURTH ANONYMOUS VOICE

Shockin' innit? It's the cuts. Tell you what, love, these days you just gotta be philosophical.

THIRD ANONYMOUS VOICE

What's that then, 'philosophical'?

FOURTH ANONYMOUS VOICE

Well, you know . . . don't think about it.

NARRATOR

And here be Ridickless, red-nosed and mouthy, with his moth-eaten brains and his tabloid tongue, trapping a punter, sounding off like a div.

RIDICKLESS

Did you 'ear, right?
They're banning black pens cause it's rashalist.
No black ink no more.
Straight up.
Ridickless, innit?
And did you 'ear?
You know yer wear black at funerals
And them undertakers
Always togged up in black and that,
And the coffins,
Always bleedin' black?
Right?
Well, they're bannin' it, ain't they?
Cause it's rashalist.
And now, right,
Yer coffin's gotta be canary yellow,
And yer undertakers' togs
And yer hearse.
Canary yellow!
Can yer believe it?
Straight up.
Ridickless, innit?

CHORUS OF ENTIRE CAST

Ridickless!

NARRATOR

And here be everyday by the way everyway
tales.

FIFTH ANONYMOUS VOICE

. . . So the bastard carves me up,
And off he goes, and I go into the kerb
And it's bollixed me underneath, and
Me uncle towed me home, and
I know you can get it done,
All straightened up on a jig,
But it costs a thousand sovs
And the whole effin' car, it only cost me a ton.
And bloody hell if that very same night
Some scumbag don't half-inch the lights,
And now the stereo's gone,
And all things considered,
Say what you like,
I've had enough,
And bloody hell,
I'd be better off with a bike.

NARRATOR

And here be paradox, workaday and winged.

FIRST ANONYMOUS VOICE

I got this dog right, and he's dead soppy right?
Soppiest dog ever, wouldn't hurt a fly,
And he loves everyone, right?
I mean everyone, right?
But if a black man come up to him,
He goes crazy, right?
Barkin' and snarlin' like somefink
You wouldn't believe.

I can't hardly hold him.
Well, what's all that about then?
That dog's black all over,
Black as coal,
Black as bleedin' night.
I say to him, 'You daft sod,
You should look in the sodding mirror, mate,
That'd give you a fright.'

NARRATOR

Martha the black cat sits on the wall and waits for catloving hapless passers-by, and way above a woman screams in Ramillies Road. She has opened the window, has filled her lungs, and she wails like a muezzin from the cloud-capped minaret of a major domestic dispute.

MARIA, THE SCREAMING GREEK

Help! Help! Help! Help! Help! . . . !

NARRATOR

The blood of Earlsfield curdles, and life stops, and everyone lifts their chin to listen. Antique Annie sits on the wall with Emphysemic Eric, Thrombotic Bert and Potty Ingrid.

ANTIQUE ANNIE

It's her again. Off she goes.

THROMBOTIC BERT

Just when it was nice and peaceful, almost time for a cuppa tea and a chocolate digestive.

POTTY INGRID

I don't know how he stands it. All that noise.

EMPHYSEMIC ERIC

Needs a good wacking, that one does.

MARIA, THE SCREAMING GREEK

Somebody! Help! Help!

NARRATOR

Antique Annie rings the doorbell and waits for the intercom voice of the man.

INTERCOM VOICE OF DESPERATE DANNY

Hello?

ANTIQUE ANNIE

Here, I've called the rozzers, 'cause-a your bloody row.

NARRATOR

NARRATOR

She returns to her place on the wall, and smiles smugly, and says

ANTIQUE ANNIE

Now watch this.

NARRATOR

And thirty seconds later the door flies open and Screaming Maria totters on high heels at high speed down Garratt Lane, and out comes Desperate Danny.

DESPERATE DANNY

Oh no, you didn't call the police! Oh no, what'm I gonna do?

ANTIQUE ANNIE

Well she shouldn't make such a bloody row, specially not on a Sunday.

THROMBOTIC BERT

At elevenses.

DESPERATE DANNY

She can't help it, she's Greek.

ALL FOUR TOGETHER

Oh, she's Greek.

NARRATOR

And here's the police slinking up in a jam sandwich, and here's the copper downwinding the glass, and here's the copper saying

COPPER

Somebody call?

ANTIQUE ANNIE

Wasn't us.

COPPER

Somebody did. Woman in extreme distress, sound of screaming, murder imminent.

DESPERATE DANNY

It was me girlfriend.

ALL FIVE TOGETHER

She's Greek.

COPPER

Drama in the blood.

ALL FIVE TOGETHER

Can't help it.

COPPER

So where's she gone?

ALL FIVE TOGETHER

Buggered off, she has, but God know's where.

DESPERATE DANNY

Back for tea, she always is.

COPPER

Ninety percent of a policeman's workload is dealing with things that didn't happen. Back to the station. Kettle's on. Sunday's the day for domestics.

NARRATOR

And there goes Ethel, prime purveyor of news and views, with her Mills and Boons and her lavender rinse and her one snout daily and her pink-rimmed specs, and her chequered bag and her practical shoes, and her wartime tales, and she's having a word with Dave, funereal and grave.

You remember Betty?
Big fat Betty who used to sit on the wall
And have a joke and a laugh and a fag
With Emphysemic Eric
Well, her toes turned black, didn't they?
And then they cut them off
And then she's diabetic, isn't she?
And she was in St George's for seven months
And they didn't feed her properly, did they?
And then her whole leg turns black
And so they cut it off,
And then the next week she gets pneumonia
Because of the shock,
And it ain't the old-fashioned kind they
Used to call the old people's friend,
It's another kind called viral,
And then she goes and dies.
And she's lived here longer than you have,
You know the woman I mean,
Big fat Betty with legs like that.

NARRATOR

And Martha the black cat, the most horrible cat
in Ramillies Road, scratcher of dogs and slayer
of all living things, lies fat and sleepy on a
further wall, waiting.

PASSER-BY

Pussy pussy pussy pussy. Isn't she sweet? What

a gorgeous cat. What lovely green eyes. Not a trace of white, what a nice bushy tail.

NARRATOR

And Martha squirms and rolls on her back as the stranger coos, and she's coy and sweet and longing for love, and the stranger outreaches a hand. And Martha flicks the tip of her tail and moves like a snake that strikes, sinks thirteen teeth and sixteen claws into innocent skin, and the stranger howls, and Martha growls.

PASSER-BY

Aaaaaaargh! Christ! Bloody hell!

THROMBOTIC BERT

Martha's bagged another one.

EMPHYSEMIC ERIC

That's the fourth today.

ANTIQUE ANNIE

She's such a minx.

DESPERATE DANNY

She's like my Greek.

Good old Martha.

ALL FIVE TOGETHER

The most horrible cat on Ramillies Road.

NARRATOR

Mr Wong feels heartburn stir, and off he goes to Mrs Rajiv's pharmacy, open on Sundays, prescriptions fulfilled, advice and smiles, no charge.

MRS RAJIV

Ah, good morning, Mr Wong, sir, and what would you like?

MR WONG

Lennies, please.

MRS RAJIV

Lennies?

MR WONG

Yes, Lennies.

Excuse me, Mr Wong, sir, but what do you mean? I have nothing at all called Lennies, isn't it.

MR WONG

Yes you do. Bad stomach. Too much chips! Jamaica pattie! Lennies! Behind you.

NARRATOR

Light dawns at last in the Rajiv pharmacy and Mrs Rajiv wags her head and smiles.

MRS RAJIV

Ah, you mean R-r-r-r-r-ennies, isn't it?

MR WONG

Yes, Lennies.

NARRATOR

And Cheryl's on her roller skates, and Mandy's got new shoes, and Posh Katy Scatty-and-Brainy comes back from the shop with the *Sunday Times* and a warm loaf, and she sings.

POSH KATY

Captain Smith and Pocahontas
Had a very mad affair.
When her daddy tried to kill him,
She said, 'Daddy, don't you dare.'
You give me fever . . .

NARRATOR

And Cheryl's eleven and full of verve, and
Mandy's eleven and full of noise, and they hear
Posh Katy sing, and hide by the hedge by the
bins.

POSH KATY

You give me fever . . .

MANDY AND CHERYL

BOO!

POSH KATY

Aagh! God, you frightened me! You little . . .

MANDY AND CHERYL
(*chanting*)

Made you jump,
Made you stare,
Made you lose you underwear.

POSH KATY

Vengeance is mine! It's Katy the Killer! Kate strikes back!

NARRATOR

Posh Katy chases the girls, darting behind the bins, and Katy wields the baguette, and it snaps on Mandy's head. The girls squeal, and the London sparrows twitter in the eves, jump from sills, and worry at crumbs.

THE LONDON SPARROWS

Tweet sodding tweet. You-git you-git-you-git-you. Tweet.

DESPERATE DANNY

Well we come out one day
And there's this sodding great truck
With a jack and a crane and a sling
And they're moving our cars up the frog.
There's a couple of rozzers mooching,
And we say

EMPHYSEMIC ERIC, THROMBOTIC BERT
AND DESPERATE DANNY

What for are you moving our cars?

DESPERATE DANNY

And they say

CHORUS OF COPPERS

Sorry, squire, it's parking markings.

DESPERATE DANNY

And we say

EMPHYSEMIC ERIC, THROMBOTIC BERT
AND DESPERATE DANNY

Parking markings?

DESPERATE DANNY

And they say

CHORUS OF COPPERS

Yes, parking markings.

DESPERATE DANNY

And we say

ALL THREE

We don't want no parking markings.
Parking's a pain as it is.

DESPERATE DANNY

And they say

CHORUS OF COPPERS

It's the council – silly sods –
Nothing better to do.
So don't blame us,
We're only doing our job.

DESPERATE DANNY

And we say

ALL THREE

Fancy a nice cuppa tea?

DESPERATE DANNY

And they say

CHORUS OF COPPERS

Can't say we mind if we do.

DESPERATE DANNY

And we sit in a row on the wall
And then these blokes roll up, right?
In them dayglo dungarees,
All spotty and splattered with grime,

Laying white lines here, and
White lines there,
All pukka and careful and neat, and
We say

What are we going to do?
Parking's a pain as it is.

DESPERATE DANNY

And Dave's a roofer, right?
And he's got a gadget for tar, and
That night Dave goes out, and
I'm watching out for the Bill, and
He burns up and blanks out the lines, and
We park up our cars like before,
The way we always did, and
We say

CHORUS OF ENTIRE CAST

Sod the council, and
Sod the parking markings -
Parking's a pain as it is.

NARRATOR

And Posh Katy Head-in-Air
Does her eyes and combs her hair.

She is
Blue-eyed and lovely.
Long in the leg,
Blonde if the sun shines,
With a weakness for shoes and Cuban heels
And a brooch in the shape of an owl.
And her mind's awhirl with troubadours,
And the arc of courtesans,
And Anna Magdalena's
Minuets in G.
And Katy's in love with a ne'er-do well
With a tangled heart and tales to tell
But Katy is sure that life is good,
And that fate would smile
Perhaps
If it could.
And Posh Katy Head-in-Air
Does her eyes and combs her hair.

The soil warms up in the deep ground, the
dead feel more at home, and a mist of loss
seeps up the burrows of the worms and settles
on the blades and roots of grass. It inches up
the trees, condenses on the stones, and on the
shoes and ankles of those who come to walk
and those who come to mourn, and the dead
philosopher cries

VOICE OF THE DEAD PHILOSOPHER

We are all forefathers of future dead.

And out walks Katy with her deadloss man, arm in arm for the epitaphs, and sorrow strokes her heart for those she never knew, and pity seeps down the burrows of the worms and settles on the scraps of wood and bone, condenses on the rosaries and wedding rings, and the clay sighs, and out walks Katy with her no-good man, and Katy cries at a child's grave that is one yard long and a hundred years of age. And the French dead speak.

VOICES OF THE FRENCH DEAD

First Voice: Ah, comme elle est belle! Comme je voudrais être au monde!
Second Voice: Ah, ses larmes qui tremblent au joues!
Third Voice: Ah, ses beaux yeaux bleus!
First Voice: Ah, ses lèvres rosâtre et douces!
Second Voice: Ah, ses mamelles pleines!
Third Voice: Ah, ses cuisses blanches!

VOICES OF THE ENGLISH DEAD

First Voice: Someone's talking foreign.
Second Voice: It's them Frenchies, off again.
Third Voice: Them Hug-you-nots.
First Voice: Hug-you-lots, more like.
Second Voice: Only think of one thing, that lot.
Third Voice: Been lyin' there three hundred years, and still goin' on about you-know-what.

First Voice: C'est la vie.

Second Voice: C'est naturel.

Third Voice: Ungrateful Rosbifs!

First Voice: We gave you jobs, we made your factories.

Second Voice: We brought you silver.

Third Voice: Nice round bellies for ze girls, mon dieu, mon dieu.

First Voice: And none of you could cook!

Second Voice: Zey have no grace, no gratitude at all!

First and Second English Voices: But we are grateful!

Third English Voice: Well I'm not.

First French Voice; Still, we get along.

Second English Voice: This is a nice cemetery.

Second French Voice: People are dying to get in.

NARRATOR

And there's one grey stone that says

ANONYMOUS VOICE

Here lies
MUM.
Thanks for all the jam tarts.

41

And there's one grey stone in the shape and form of a toy bear, and the legend mourns:

VOICE OF THE BEREAVED IRISH MOTHER

In loving memory of our baby son, Michael Joseph, died at birth.

NARRATOR

And every day,
Loyal like shadows,
Faithful like sun,
Pale as the March moon,
Here she comes with a new bloom
And a nightlight lit in the silver lamp.
And so she stands and so she smokes,
And so she imagines,
And so she yearns,
And so she gazes down.

VOICE OF BEREAVED IRISH MOTHER

Our baby son, Michael Joseph, died at birth.

NARRATOR

Down at the railway station Darren and Alan, six years old, bullet-headed boys with old mens' eyes, are running the railway scam.

Here mister, finished wiv yer travel card? Give
you a quid.

Here missus, wanna buy a travelcard? Two
quid.

And Martha waits on the wall, and a siren wails
and recedes, and Danny looks up and recalls

Remember when Bert was ill,
And he needed a lift to the doc?
And we asked Fagin, we said

Bert needs a lift to the Doc.

And Fagin says

Well, I would, but this car belongs to me bird,
And she wouldn't like it.

And we say

CHORUS OF WALLSITTERS

Bert's ill.

DESPERATE DANNY

And he says

FAGIN

I would, but this car belongs to me bird.

DESPERATE DANNY

So anyway, one day, Fagin's come back with
his bird,
And he's parking up by the kerb,
And Dave's got a smoke-bomb, right?
And he slips it under the car,
And the car's all filling with smoke,
And Fagin leaps out and he's running,
Waving his arms like a prat,
Like he's leaving his bird there to burn,
And she's just sitting there,
And for all he knows,
He's only left her to burn.
Laugh? Laugh?
Bloody Nora, mate, me and Bert and Dave

We very nearly pissed ourselves.

CHORUS OF MANDY, CHERYL, ALAN
AND DARREN

Mary had a little lamb
She also had a duck
She put them on the mantelpiece
To see if they would make friends.

NARRATOR

Under the railway bridge that drips with last
night's rain, a hundred low-life doves adorn the
girders, and those beneath walk faster for fear
of muck-in-hair and streaks on sleeves, and
everyone's complaining to the council, but
nothing's ever done.

ANTIQUE ANNIE

It's a disgrace.

MRS WONG

Hollible! Hollible!

POTTY INGRID

They've got to live somewhere. Poor darlings!

THROMBOTIC BERT

Slime on the pavement.

EMPHYSEMIC ERIC

Rats on wings. Death and disease and God-knows-what.

NARRATOR

And Desperate Danny's got more news, the greatest latest of Ramillies Road.

DESPERATE DANNY

So I'm coming outa the alley.
It's a nice day,
Currant bun,
Not much wind.
And there's Dave,
And he's coming out of his house,
And I stop and look,
And I look twice,
And it's just as I thought,
'Cause behind him there's only a horse,
And I say, 'Blimey Dave, what's that?'
And he says

DAVE

That's Nobby.

And I say, 'It's a horse.'
And he says

DAVE

Course it's a horse.

DESPERATE DANNY

And I say 'You livin' with that?'
And he says

DAVE

No, I live with my wife,
This one lives in the yard,
And I bring 'im out through the house,
And we go for a walk in the park.

DESPERATE DANNY

And I say, 'So it's really a bit like a dog?'
And he says

DAVE

Nah, this is cheaper,
Worked it all out I did.
Bale of straw lasts a week, right?
And it only costs two quid.

Mary had a little lamb
She put it in a bucket
When it jumped right out again
She said 'O bother!'

NARRATOR

Down at the stadium-market in the pose of
Hamlet cradling Yorick's skull, Honest Phil
takes up a toaster, clears his throat and claims

HONEST PHIL

Nah this is fifty quid in the shops, straight up,
but I'm not asking fifty quid. In fact I'm not
even asking forty quid, let alone forty-five. I'm
not after thirty-five, and I don't want thirty
either. When it comes down to it I'm not even
going to flog it for twenty. Believe it or not
ladies and gentlemen, I can scarce believe it
myself, I am offering this toaster for a tenner.
Only a mere tenner. All brand new stuff. Look
at all that chrome, high quality. You know
where I am, I'm here every week, unconditional
guarantee, you don't like it, you bring it back.
Who'll take a fine pukka toaster for a tenner?
That lady over there! See, someone's got some
sense. It's reassuring, that is. And that gentleman over there, he's not handsome but he's not
stupid neither. A toaster for the gentleman!

48

Back in Earlsfield Mrs Wong puts on the chips, and the fume of palm-fat weights the air, and the sun comes out, and Garratt Lane booms to the heavy bass of youths in cars with windows down. The locals tut and curl their lips, and peace is gone as the windows shake and patience dims.

ANTIQUE ANNIE

Bloody racket. Didn't do that when we was young.

POTTY INGRID

No consideration.

THROMBOTIC BERT

Drives you barmy.

MR AND MRS WONG

Hollible! Hollible!

EMPHYSEMIC ERIC

If it was music, wouldn't be so bad.

NARRATOR

And Parachute Sam, elite but unemployed, with

his red beret and his khaki fatigues, fresh from Fantasy Action Land, puts down his SS mag and lifts the sash and scowls. The bass booms as the lights turn red, and Sam sees red. Sam is alone in his dormer room, and he strokes his 'tache and adjusts his eyes and spots the youth with his jazzed-up car and his Rayban shades, and his shaven skull and arm outside who nods his head to the braindeath bass. And Sam's on fire with the rage of the noise, for all he wants is the peace and quiet to get to grips with war. Now Sam's at the sill with his box of stones and his great crusade and his Black Widow cattie (not to be sold to children, designed for pest control) and 'zing' goes the cattie and a stone sings and the stone dings, and one more noisy poser gets a nasty shock and a dent. He stares around with a wild surmise and the lights change and people toot and off he goes. Sam smiles and squares his chest, puts the catapult by, a warrior down to the bones. Now Sam goes back to his mag and Sam's a Spetznatz and Sam's in the SAS and Sam's in the Royal Marines and Sam is Beau Sabreur. And Martha lies on the wall and bags another passer-by.

PASSER-BY

Puddy puddy puddy . . . Aaargh, bloody Nora!

The most horrible cat in Ramillies Road!

NARRATOR

And here comes Ethel, prime surveyor of news
and views, with her Mills and Boon, her one
snout daily, her pink-rimmed specs, her
lavender rinse and her gingham bag, her
complaints to the council, and her practical
shoes.

ETHEL

I see you've got that black man moved in next
door,
He's alcoholic, that's what they're saying.
I sold him two bottles of scotch
A fiver each
I didn't want 'em,
And bother me if they weren't both in the bin
The morning after.
But he's harmless.
And you've got them Albanian refugees
I know
I heard their dodgy music
Had the window open, didn't they?
I see Fagin's moved out
But he's only over the road, he ain't gone far
I'm glad about that
You get used to your neighbours, don't you?

The London sparrows are scrapping for seed, and the urban foxes, smart and respectable, yawn by the graves while Thrombotic Bert relates the tale of John and Queenie the dog.

THROMBOTIC BERT

So I looked out of me window, right, and there's John up to his knees in my flower bed, digging a bloody great hole. And there's me gladioli and me daff bulbs and me lilies and me polys scattered all over the place, and a sodding great heap of clay getting bigger by the spadeful on the path, so I says 'Bloody 'ell, what's 'e up to, the silly sod?' and I was right annoyed, like. So I runs out and says 'What the effin' 'eck are you doing in my flower bed, diggin' that bloody great hole?' and John looks up, and 'e can 'ardly speak, and there's tears in his eyes, and he just says

JOHN

'Queenie's dead.'

THROMBOTIC BERT

And I think 'Queenie? Queenie?' and then I remember it's his dog. Remember John's dog? Little skinny black thing, so pop-eyed from constipation it had a hump from trying to do its business while it walked, and him just tugging it along all the way to the Sailor Prince so it never got a chance. And anyway, he loved that dog, it was all he had, like, and he lived all alone apart from the dog, and he hardly spoke 'cause he was so out of practice, and when he did speak it was always 'effin' this, and 'effin' that because 'e'd forgotten all the other words and couldn't remember them unless he said 'effin' first.

Anyway, I felt sorry for him, like, cause Queenie was his whole world, and I couldn't feel angry, and I said, 'Well, I'm sorry about that, John, but why are you digging to bloody Australia in my flower bed?' and he says

JOHN

Fu . . . fu . . . fu . . . fuckin', 'cause I ain't got nowhere to fuckin' bury her.

THROMBOTIC BERT

and I realise he's going to bury it in my flowerbed without even askin'. But he's so upset I just resign myself.

So anyway, the next Sunday I look out of me window, and there's old John, still crying, and he's building a nice little wall round the flower bed, and a few days later there's a stone from the Co-op funeral parlour set up in the middle, and it says

'My dog Queenie'

THROMBOTIC BERT

on it, and every day he stands there for a while, lookin' down on Queenie. And I planted it all up nice, and when I look at it now I remember poor old John dragging Queenie on a string, down to the Sailor Prince.

EMPHYSEMIC ERIC

What happened to him? I ain't seen him for ages.

ANTIQUE ANNIE

Brown Bread. Cancer. So when he was diagnosed he went down to the pub every night and he akcherly started talking, and he made friends for the first time, and he reeled home at closing time all at sixes and sevens and when he passed the flowerbed he said

JOHN

Goodnight, Queenie. You was a good old girl.

ANTIQUE ANNIE

and he was just like a bleedin' skelenten, and all his hair came out so he had to wear a hat, and then one day no one had seed him for three days, and they broke down his door and there he was, all but dead, and then he died, and I ain't got a clue where they buried him. We wasn't told. And then this woman turns up sayin' she's his sister, and she goes through his stuff and takes everything worth having, which wasn't much, she says she never saw him for forty years, the cow, and akcherly asks if he had any other relatives, and then they turn out his things, which weren't even good enough for Oxfam, and that's him, dead and forgot, and only Queenie's grave to remind us by.

ALL THREE TOGETHER

Poor old sod.

NARRATOR

Poor John in a chipboard box in a pauper's grave in a corner by the railway-side, amid the ochre bones of strangers, dreams of Queenie and remembers

JOHN

Fu . . . fu . . . fu . . . fuckin', she were a good old girl.

NARRATOR

Under the lilies Queenie thinks of John, and
Bert complains

THROMBOTIC BERT

Now there's two fat Glasgow Scotch birds in
John's old room, and they 'ave four different
men every night each.

EMPHYSEMIC ERIC

They're havin' a competition.

ANTIQUE ANNIE

And they don't use bins, just chuck their
rubbish out the window, bloody aerosols
everywhere.

EMPHYSEMIC ERIC

Bloody Scotch. All drunks with ginger bollocks.

THROMBOTIC BERT

And that's just the women.

ANTIQUE ANNIE

My mum was Scotch.

EMPHYSEMIC ERIC AND THROMBOTIC BERT

No offence.

ANTIQUE ANNIE

None taken.

EMPHYSEMIC ERIC

Me old lady's waving from the window.

THROMBOTIC BERT

Cushty. Time for roast with gravy.

ANTIQUE ANNIE

Frozen peas.

EMPHYSEMIC ERIC

Sec you later.

THROMBOTIC BERT

Baked potayter.

EMPHYSEMIC ERIC

Baked.

Up in King George's Park the white-clad oldies clock a final game of bowls, oblivious yuppies gambol on the courts, and bullet-headed boys and grubby-knickered girls, pre-prandial rhymester-laureates of the roundabouts and swings, extemporise a verse:

CHORUS OF CHILDREN

Little Miss Muffet
Sat on a tuffet
Wiv 'er knickers all tattered and torn.
It wasn't the spider
That sat down beside her,
But Little Boy Blue,
With his horn.

NARRATOR

The children whoop and laugh and leave. It's almost lunchtime and the silent anonymous yuppies make pasta with pesto in their first house on the ladder, drifting like wraiths and shadows through winebars and through longer locals' lives. Katy chops veg with a blunt knife, the boyfriend fries, and Katy sings

Fever! In the morning
Fever all through the night,
You give me fever.

NARRATOR

The normal folk do Sunday roast, Mrs Wong
does saveloys, the black cats sleep on sills. The
urban foxes, smart and respectable, yawn by
the graves where the dead doze, and down in
the Wandle there's dace and a heron and
another Sainsbury trolley, and a broken bike.
The blue plastic bags arrive in Tooting Bec, the
familiar sun ponders the panopticon of
Wandsworth nick, a rat fusses and furbishes on
the allotment, and these are the morning's
messages in Tippex and marker and sprays of
paint, these are the signs of the times behind the
Henry Prince estate.

On the seat it says

FIRST ANONYMOUS TEENAGER

'Small-breasted girls
Have the biggest hearts, like Tracey.'

NARRATOR

And on the bridge it says

'Carly and Ruth –
We are the crazy girls.'

NARRATOR

And on the seat it says

ASHLEY

'Ashley for Simone.'

NARRATOR

And on the bin it says

SECOND ANONYMOUS TEENAGER

'For dogpoo only.'

NARRATOR

And on the bridge it says

ANY VOICE

'Why don't you love me?'

NARRATOR

And in the river is a rocking horse,
Topped off with a moorhen's nest,
And starlings flee,

As two kestrels
Fly out above the factory.

The streets grow still,
The day's unfurled;
In Sunday noonday Earlsfield
At the centre of the world.

FINIS

Louis de Bernières

THE WAR OF DON EMMANUEL'S NETHER PARTS

'A very good book indeed, the sharpest and
funniest I have read in quite some time'
Financial Times

When the haughty Don Constanza tries to
divert a river to fill her swimming pool, she
starts a running battle with the locals. The
skirmishes are so severe that the government
dispatches a squadron of soldiers led by the
fat, brutal and stupid Figueras to deal with
them.

Despite visiting plagues of laughing fits and
giant cats upon the troops, the villagers know
that to escape the cruel and unusual tortures
planned for them, they must run. Thus they
plan to head for the mountains and start a
new and convivial civilisation.

'A tour de force' *Time Out*

VINTAGE

Louis de Bernières

SEÑOR VIVO AND THE COCA LORD

Dionisio Vivo, a young South American
lecturer in philosophy, is puzzled by the
hideously mutilated corpses that keep turning
up outside his front door. To his friend,
Ramon, one of the few honest policemen in
town, the message is all too clear: Dionisio's
letters to the press, exposing the drug barons,
must stop; and although Dionisio manages to
escape the hit-men sent to get him, he soon
realises that others are more vulnerable, and
his love for them leads him to take a colossal
revenge.

'Sharp, funny, engaging and British . . . de
Bernières is doing for Colombia's drug culture
what Tom Wharpe did for apartheid. His
approach is flippant, but the purpose behind it
is deadly serious.'
Financial Times

VINTAGE

Louis de Bernières

THE TROUBLESOME OFFSPRING OF CARDINAL GUZMAN

While the economy of his small South American country collapses, President Veracruz joins his improbable populace of ex-soldiers, former guerillas, unfrocked priests and reformed – though by no means inactive – whores, in a bizarre search for sexual fulfilment.

But for Cardinal Guzman, a man tormented by his own private daemons, their stupendous, hedonistic fiestas represent the epicentre of all heresies. Heresies that must be challenged with a horrifying new inquisition destined to climax in a spectacular confrontation.

'An extraordinary feat of imagination . . . A sensuous, often farcical and ultimately optimistic argument for spiritual sanity'
Time Out

VINTAGE

Louis de Bernières

CAPTAIN CORELLI'S MANDOLIN

It is 1941 and Captain Antonio Corelli, a young Italian officer, is posted to the Greek island of Cephallonia as part of the occupying forces. At first he is ostracised by the locals, but as a conscientious but far from fanatical soldier, whose main aim is to have a peaceful war, he proves in time to be civilised, humorous – and a consummate musician.

When the local doctor's daughter's letters to her fiancé – a member of the underground – go unanswered, the working of the eternal triangle seems inevitable. But can this fragile love survive as a war of bestial savagery gets closer and the lines are drawn between invader and defender?

'A true diamond of a novel, glinting with comedy and tragedy'
Daily Mail

VINTAGE

BY LOUIS DE BERNIERES

ALSO AVAILABLE IN VINTAGE

The War of Don Emmanuel's Nether Parts	£6.99
Señor Vivo and the Coca Lord	£6.99
The Troublesome Offspring of Cardinal Guzman	£6.99
Captain Corelli's Mandolin	£6.99

- All Vintage books are available through mail order or from your local bookshop.

- Payment may be made using Access, Visa, Mastercard, Diners Club, Switch and Amex, or cheque, eurocheque and postal order (sterling only).

☐☐☐☐☐☐☐☐☐☐☐☐☐☐☐☐

Expiry Date:_____ Signature:_____

Please allow £2.50 for post and packing for the first book and £1.00 per book thereafter.

ALL ORDERS TO:
Vintage Books, Books by Post, TBS Limited, The Book Service,
Colchester Road, Frating Green, Colchester, Essex, CO7 7DW, UK.
Telephone: (01206) 256 000
Fax: (01206) 255 914

NAME:_____

ADDRESS:_____

_____

_____

Please allow 28 days for delivery. Please tick box if you do not
wish to receive any additional information   ☐
Prices and availability subject to change without notice.